Beebs Cooks a Turkey!

by Donald W. Kruse

Beebs Cooks a Turkey! by Donald W. Kruse, Illustrations by Billy Barron is published by:

ZACCHEUS ENTERTAINMENT

Beebs Cooks a Turkey! Copyright © 2016 by Donald W. Kruse

All rights reserved worldwide, including the right to reproduce this book or portions thereof in any form whatsoever. For comments or questions write to:
Zaccheus Entertainment
P.O. Box 7427
Prospect Heights, IL 60070
ISBN: 978-0-99699-643-3

Manufactured in the United States of America

A special thank you from the author to Billy Barron

Cover and interior illustrations by Billy Barron

OTHER BOOKS BY DONALD W. KRUSE

Jasper Has Left the Building!

Jasper Has Returned!

Jasper And The Haunted House!

Hey, Charlie!

Fleas, Please!

Gorilla Soup!

Pee-Pee Harley and the Bandit!

Where's the Gold?

Dear Joey

Ragdolly's Love

Moose Pee and Tea!

That's Not a Pickle! Parts 1 through 7

What Do You Feed a Snow Snoot?

Monster at O'Malley's Mansion

Cluck, Cluck, Cluck … SPLASH!

There's a Goof on My Roof!

Waldo, Blue, and Glad Max Too!

Blitz and Blatz!

Beebs Goes Camping!

To

my grandson Colin who really does

know how to cook!

INTRODUCTION

Kruse doesn't have to change the spelling to be a star.

He's there already with his wonderful, bizarre tale of a naked turkey.

May he and his bird realize the sky's the limit.

—Ed Asner

This is Beebs …

Beebs is my grandpa. I named him Beebs when I was only two years old because he's not just my grandpa … he's my very own special friend.

Beebs is very kind and thoughtful. He spends a lot of time with me, and I love him very much.

But ...

Beebs has a problem.

He's always getting into some kind of trouble.

And I'm always there to help poor Beebs in any way I can.

On Thanksgiving Day, Grandma reminded Beebs—in her own special way—that it was Beebs' turn to cook the turkey because last year Beebs had complained to Grandma that her turkey was too dry and not juicy.

Then Beebs shrugged his shoulders and said to me, "I think I'll cook a turkey today."

And of course, I stayed in the kitchen to help.

First, Beebs tied Grandma's apron around his waist. Then he put on his chef's hat.

So far ... so good, I thought.

Then Beebs removed a tiny, little pan from the cabinet and said, "We'll cook our turkey in this."

"How big is the turkey?" I asked.

"Twenty-two pounds," Beebs replied.

"But, Beebs," I said. And before I could say another word, Beebs disappeared into the pantry to fetch ingredients for our turkey.

Suddenly Beebs yelled at the top of his lungs, "OUCH! OUCH! OUCH! OUCH!" Then he turned around, holding up his hand.

Stuck on the end of his finger was a mouse trap!

"Beebs!" I cried. "Are you all right?"

"I'm all right. I'm allll right," said Beebs, gritting his teeth.

After I removed the mouse trap from Beebs' finger, he went back to the pantry and came out with flour, cooking oil, and lots of spices.

"Do you know what you're doing, Beebs?" I asked.

Beebs smiled confidently. "Believe it or not, *I* am cooking a turkey for Thanksgiving."

Suddenly, we heard a strange, muffled bumping sound ... Boomp! Boomp! Boomp!

"Shh!" said Beebs, cocking his head, straining to hear. "What's that noise?"

We waited …

15

The noise grew louder … Boomp! Boomp!
Boomp!

"There it is again!" Beebs whispered. Then he
snatched a rubber turkey baster from the counter.

"I think it's coming from the freezer," I
whispered back.

Beebs turned to me and said, "Shh! " Then
he tiptoed to the freezer and carefully grabbed
the handle, while raising the baster in his other
hand—ready with his rubber club.

Then, just as Beebs was about to open the
freezer door …

Boomp!

The noise scared Beebs so much, he jumped right out of his shoes and flew into the pantry.

And I dove under the kitchen table—just in case!

Then …

Boomp! Boomp! Boomp!

Just then, Grandma walked into the kitchen and asked, "What in the world is making that noise?"

Then, before Beebs or I could warn her, Grandma grabbed the freezer door handle and yanked it open.

Suddenly a blue, twenty-two pound, cross-eyed, plucked turkey burst from the freezer, furiously squawking and gobbling, and flew into Grandma's head, blasting her hair curlers all over the kitchen.

"Aahhh!" Grandma screamed, frantically swatting with both hands at the cold, bare bird.

The frantic turkey flew from Grandma's head and into the pantry with Beebs.

"Aahhh!" Beebs screamed, then crashed into the shelves, knocking over boxes, bottles, and cans of food.

Then Beebs stumbled out of the pantry and tripped over a kitchen chair—boom! Beebs was down, and the dishwasher door dropped open when Beebs crashed onto the floor.

The frightened turkey was right behind Beebs, squawking and gobbling and furiously flapping its naked wings.

The freezing, frantic turkey hopped into the dishwasher and ran in circles, gobbling and squawking and fluttering its plucked wings.

"Get that turkey out of my dishwasher!" Grandma yelled, pointing at it. A few straggler hair curlers still hung from her messed up hair.

"I'm on it, Dear," Beebs replied, still sprawled on the floor.

Suddenly the turkey sprang from the dishwasher and landed on Grandma's shoulder.

"Turkey!" Grandma blurted, her eyes rolling into the back of her head. "Big turkey!"

It was too much excitement for Grandma, and she fainted on a kitchen chair.

Then the turkey fluttered from Grandma's shoulder and flew back into the dishwasher.

"Gobble! Gobble! Gobble!"

Beebs struggled up from the floor, covered in spilled food and spices.

I crawled out from under the table. "Are you all right, Beebs?" I asked, while fanning Grandma with a dish towel.

"I'm all right. I'm alllll right," said Beebs, shaking rice out of his ears.

Grandma woke up and sputtered, "Big! Big turkey!"

"Are you all right, Grandma?" I asked.

"Big turkey scared me!" Grandma blurted.

The turkey poked its head out of the dishwasher and looked at us through its crossed eyes. Then it wrapped its naked wings around itself and shivered.

"Gobble! Gobble! Gobble!"

31

"I think he's cold, Beebs," I said. "See how his knees are shaking?"

"Well, he has no feathers and he just came out of the freezer," said Beebs. "He *must* be cold—the poor fella."

"Big turkey scared me!" Grandma repeated, her eyes as big as saucers. Then she wrapped her arms protectively around me.

"What'll we do now, Beebs?" I asked.

Suddenly the turkey flew from the dishwasher and landed on the spinning ceiling fan above us, squawking like a bird gone mad!

"There he goes!" I yelled.

Just then, the spinning turkey was thrown from the fan, shooting through the air like a missile, heading toward the living room.

Beebs sprang from the kitchen, leaped over the sofa, launching himself into the air, trying to catch the turkey missile.

He missed!

The turkey plunked headfirst into our fish bowl, splashing water and goldfish everywhere!

Poor Beebs landed in a heap on the living room floor.

"Are you all right, Beebs?" I asked.

"I'm all right. I'm alllll right," said Beebs, picking himself up and brushing himself off.

Then he carefully removed the sputtering turkey from the fish bowl. "Gotcha!" he cried.

But Beebs didn't have the bird for long.

The dazed and cross-eyed turkey suddenly burst from Beebs' arms and flew smack dab into Grandma's three cats—Paws, Claws, and Jaws.

"Uh, oh," said Beebs.

At first, the cats just stared for a moment in disbelief at the helpless turkey. But then …

Paws growled.

Claws extended his weaponry on all fours.

Jaws licked his lips.

39

Just as the three cats pounced, Beebs tried to scoop up the turkey. But he missed because the turkey had shot straight up into the air, clinging to the chandelier above, safely out of the way.

But poor Beebs found himself suddenly in the middle of a cat fight—cat fur flying every which way among hisses, growls … and Beeb's screams. What a mess!

Finally I was able to shoo the cats away, and Beebs stood up, checking for scratches.

"Are you all right, Beebs?" I asked.

"I'm all right. I'm alllll right," said Beebs.

Just then, the *turkey* fainted and dropped from the chandelier into Beebs' arms.

"It must've been too much excitement for him, Beebs," I said.

"This is one cold bird," said Beebs. "We better get him some clothes before he freezes to death."

"But Beebs," I said.

And before I could say another word, Beebs carried the fainted turkey upstairs to get it some clothes.

Beebs carefully dressed the turkey in a ski hat, a scarf, tee-shirt, shorts, socks, and mittens. Then he carefully dabbed its face with cold water, waking up the fainted bird.

The warmed turkey uncrossed its eyes and was very happy when it discovered its new clothes.

"Gobble! Gobble! Gobble!"

Later, we all sat at the dinner table and ate our Thanksgiving dinner. We ate macaroni and cheese, hot dogs, and corn-on-the-cob.

Grandma cooked it, and of course, it was deeeeelicious!

And the turkey thought so, too!

"Gobble! Gobble! Gobble!"

And even though I didn't get any turkey, I still spent time with Beebs and Grandma, and it was the best Thanksgiving I ever had!

CPSIA information can be obtained at www.ICGtesting.com
Printed in the USA
LVOW09s0321100516

487478LV00002B/2/P